TRIALS AND BAD GUYS

COLORING BOOK

Travis Holter and Nicholas Baer

"I'd like to dedicate this work to those who never stopped believing in me, and my dreams, even when I stopped. To those who urged me to draw, to create, even when I didn't feel like it. Thank you for all the support—I wouldn't be here without all of you. And with your continued support, I'll continue creating works that I hope will inspire others and spark their imaginations."

— Nick Baer

Half Orc Archer

Race Info:

Once per fight, Half-Orcs get to deal an extra 5 damage on a hit.

Class Info:

Once per fight, archers can shoot twice on one turn.

Name:

____

Race: Half-Orc
Class: Archer
Armor: 18
Health: 22

Attack
1d20+9 —> 1d10

Stuff:

Leather Armor, Bow

Half Orc Archer

Race Info:

Once per fight, Half-Orcs get to deal an extra 5 damage on a hit.

Class Info:

Once per fight, archers can shoot twice on one turn.

Name:

____

Race: Half-Orc
Class: Archer
Armor: 18
Health: 22

Stuff:

Leather Armor, Bow

<u>Attack</u>

1d20+9 —> 1d10

Half Orc Barbarian

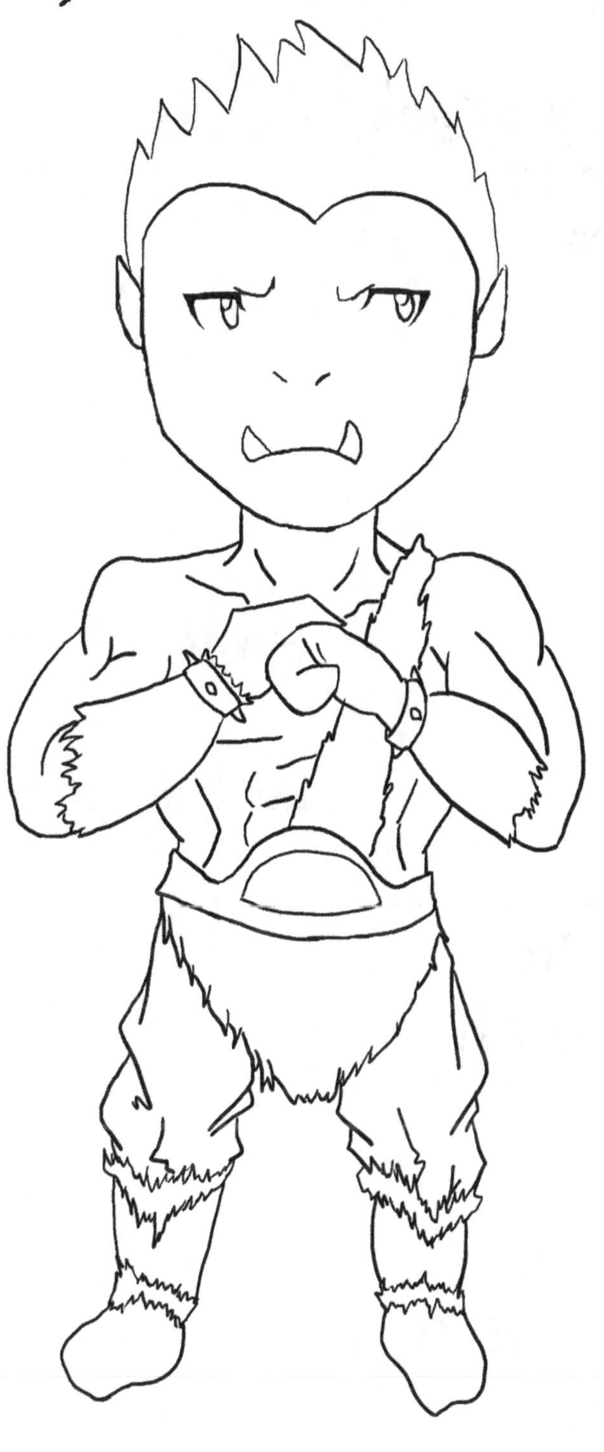

____

Race Info:

Once per fight, Half-Orcs get to deal an extra 5 damage on a hit.

Class Info:

-

Name:

____

Race: Half-Orc
Class: Barbarian
Armor: 17
Health: 31
<u>Attack</u>
1d20+8 —> 1d10+8

Stuff:

Leather Armor

Half Orc Barbarian

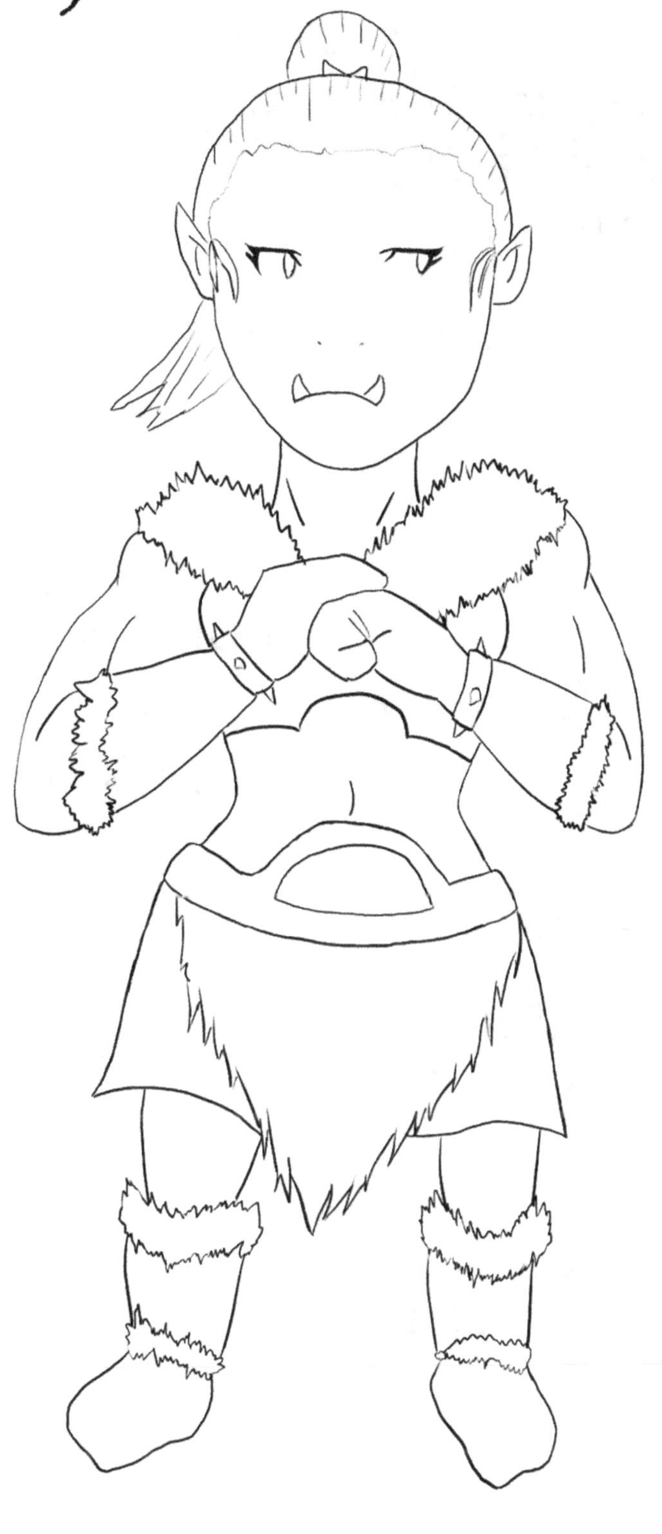

____

Race Info:	Class Info:
Once per fight, Half-Orcs get to deal an extra 5 damage on a hit.	-

Name:	Stuff:
	Leather Armor

____

Race: Half-Orc
Class: Barbarian
Armor: 17
Health: 31

Attack

1d20+8 —> 1d10+8

Half Orc Healer

Race Info:

Once per fight, Half-Orcs get to deal an extra 5 damage on a hit.

Class Info:

Instead of attacking, healers can **heal** a friend within 5 squares by **10 health**. You can do this **3 times per day**.

Name:

Stuff:

Magic Jewel

____

Race: Half-Orc
Class: Healer
Armor: 16
Health: 22
<u>Attack</u>
1d20+5 —> 1d8+3

Half Orc Healer

Race Info:

Once per fight, Half-Orcs get to deal an extra 5 damage on a hit.

Class Info:

Instead of attacking, healers can **heal** a friend within 5 squares by **10 health**. You can do this **3 times per day**.

Name:

____

Race: Half-Orc
Class: Healer
Armor: 16
Health: 22

<u>Attack</u>

1d20+5 —> 1d8+3

Stuff:

Magic Jewel

Half Orc Paladin

Race Info:

Once per fight, Half-Orcs get to deal an extra 5 damage on a hit.

Class Info:

Instead of attacking, paladins can **challenge** a bad guy next to them. That bad guy may only attack you and has to leave your friends alone. It lasts until you challenge someone else, or the fight ends.

Name:

Stuff:

Metal Armor, Sword

____

Race: Half-Orc

Class: Healer

Armor: 20

Health: 35

Attack

1d20+7 —> 1d8+3

Half Orc Paladin

Race Info:

Once per fight, Half-Orcs get to deal an extra 5 damage on a hit.

Class Info:

Instead of attacking, paladins can **challenge** a bad guy next to them. That bad guy may only attack you and has to leave your friends alone. It lasts until you challenge someone else, or the fight ends.

Name:

____

Race: Half-Orc
Class: Healer
Armor: 20
Health: 35

<u>Attack</u>

1d20+7 —> 1d8+3

Stuff:

Metal Armor, Sword

Half Orc Thief

____

Race Info:

Once per fight, Half-Orcs get to deal an extra 5 damage on a hit.

Class Info:

If the bad guy you hit has one of your friends on the other side of it you get **backstab bonus, +2d6 extra damage.**

Thieves are the only class that can **pick locks.**

Name:

____

Race: Half-Orc

Class: Thief

Armor: 16

Health: 23

<u>Attack</u>

1d20+8 —> 1d6+5

Stuff:

Leather Armor, Dagger, Lockpicks

Half Orc Thief

Race Info:

Once per fight, Half-Orcs get to deal an extra 5 damage on a hit.

Class Info:

If the bad guy you hit has one of your friends on the other side of it you get **backstab bonus, +2d6 extra damage.**

Thieves are the only class that can **pick locks.**

Name:

____

Race: Half-Orc
Class: Thief
Armor: 16
Health: 23

Attack

1d20+8 —> 1d6+5

Stuff:

Leather Armor, Dagger, Lockpicks

Half Orc Wizard

Race Info:

Once per fight, Half-Orcs get to deal an extra 5 damage on a hit.

Class Info:

Instead of attacking, wizards can **curse** a bad guy up to 10 squares away. Cursed bad guys have
-2 armor and -2 damage for the rest of the fight.

Name:

____

Race: Half-Orc

Class: Wizard

Armor: 11

Health: 18

Attack

1d20+7 —> 1d6+5

+ 5 Splash Damage!

Stuff:

Robe, Staff,
Big Feathered Hat

Half Orc Wizard

Race Info:

Once per fight, Half-Orcs get to deal an extra 5 damage on a hit.

Class Info:

Instead of attacking, wizards can **curse** a bad guy up to 10 squares away. Cursed bad guys have
-2 armor and -2 damage for the rest of the fight.

Name:

____

Race: Half-Orc
Class: Wizard
Armor: 11
Health: 18

<u>Attack</u>

1d20+7 —> 1d6+5
+ 5 Splash Damage!

Stuff:

Robe, Staff,
Big Feathered Hat

Elf Archer

____

Race Info:

Once per fight, elves get to re-roll an attack that they missed.

Class Info:

Once per fight, archers can shoot twice on one turn.

Name:

____

Race: Elf
Class: Archer
Armor: 18
Health: 22

Stuff:

Leather Armor, Bow

Attack

1d20+9 —> 1d10

Elf Archer

Race Info:

Once per fight, elves get to re-roll an attack that they missed.

Class Info:

Once per fight, archers can shoot twice on one turn.

Name:

Stuff:

Leather Armor, Bow

____

Race: Elf
Class: Archer
Armor: 18
Health: 22

Attack

1d20+9 —> 1d10

Elf Barbarian

____

Race Info:	Class Info:
Once per fight, elves get to re-roll an attack that they missed.	-

Name:	Stuff:
	Leather Armor

Race: Elf
Class: Barbarian
Armor: 17
Health: 31

Attack
1d20+8 —> 1d10+8

Elf Barbarian

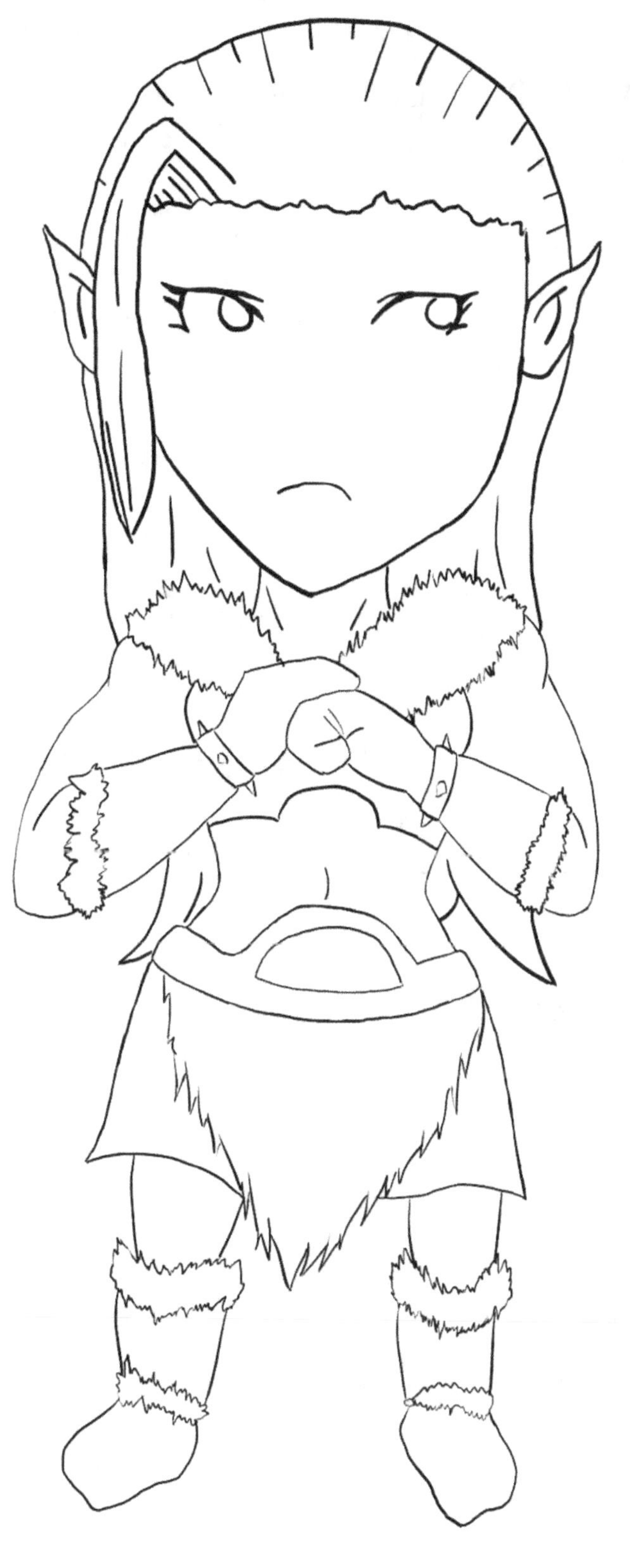

Race Info:

Once per fight, elves get to re-roll an attack that they missed.

Class Info:

-

Name:

Stuff:

Leather Armor

____

Race: Elf
Class: Barbarian
Armor: 17
Health: 31

Attack

1d20+8 —> 1d10+8

Elf Healer

Race Info:

Once per fight, elves get to re-roll an attack that they missed.

Class Info:

Instead of attacking, healers can **heal** a friend within 5 squares by **10 health.** You can do this **3 times per day.**

Name:

____

Race: Elf
Class: Healer
Armor: 16
Health: 22

Stuff:

Magic Jewel

Attack
1d20+5 —> 1d8+3

Elf Healer

____

Race Info:

Once per fight, elves get to re-roll an attack that they missed.

Class Info:

Instead of attacking, healers can **heal** a friend within 5 squares by **10 health.** You can do this **3 times per day.**

Name:

____

Race: Elf

Class: Healer

Armor: 16

Health: 22

Stuff:

Magic Jewel

Attack

1d20+5 —> 1d8+3

Elf Paladin

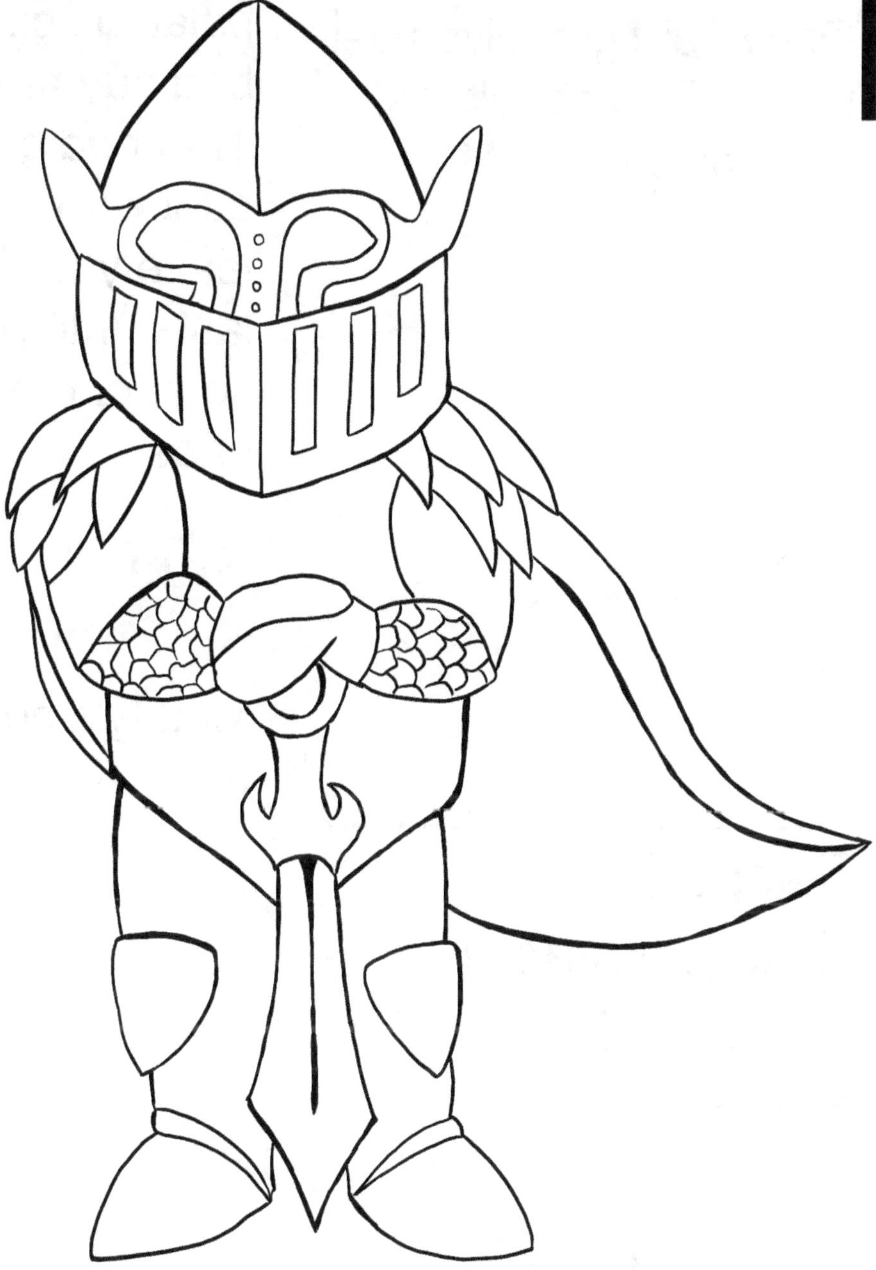

____

Race Info:

Once per fight, elves get to re-roll an attack that they missed.

Class Info:

Instead of attacking, paladins can **challenge** a bad guy next to them. That bad guy may only attack you and has to leave your friends alone. It lasts until you challenge someone else, or the fight ends.

Name:

____

Race: Elf
Class: Paladin
Armor: 20
Health: 35

Stuff:

Metal Armor, Sword

Attack
1d20+7 —> 1d8+3

Elf Thief

____

Race Info:

Once per fight, elves get to re-roll an attack that they missed.

Class Info:

If the bad guy you hit has one of your friends on the other side of it you get **backstab bonus, +2d6 extra damage.**

Thieves are the only class that can **pick locks.**

Name:

____

Race: Elf

Class: Thief

Armor: 16

Health: 23

Attack

1d20+8 —> 1d6+5

Stuff:

Leather Armor, Dagger, Lockpicks

Elf Thief

____

Race Info:

Once per fight, elves get to re-roll an attack that they missed.

Class Info:

If the bad guy you hit has one of your friends on the other side of it you get **backstab bonus, +2d6 extra damage.**

Thieves are the only class that can **pick locks.**

Name:

____

Race: Elf
Class: Thief
Armor: 16
Health: 23
<u>Attack</u>
1d20+8 —> 1d6+5

Stuff:

Leather Armor, Dagger, Lockpicks

Elf Wizard

____

Race Info:

Once per fight, elves get to re-roll an attack that they missed.

Class Info:

Instead of attacking, wizards can **curse** a bad guy up to 10 squares away. Cursed bad guys have
-2 armor and -2 damage for the rest of the fight.

Name:

____

Race: Elf

Class: Wizard

Armor: 11

Health: 18

Attack

1d20+7 —> 1d6+5

+5 Splash Damage!

Stuff:

Robe, Staff, Big Feathered Hat

Elf Wizard

Race Info:

Once per fight, elves get to re-roll an attack that they missed.

Class Info:

Instead of attacking, wizards can **curse** a bad guy up to 10 squares away. Cursed bad guys have
-2 armor and -2 damage for the rest of the fight.

Name:

____

Race: Elf

Class: Wizard

Armor: 11

Health: 18

Attack

1d20+7 —> 1d6+5

+5 Splash Damage!

Stuff:

Robe, Staff, Big Feathered Hat

HUMAN ARCHER

Race Info:

Once per day you can make a **healing potion**, if you find medicinal herbs.

OR

Once per day you can use magic to **stun everyone** within two squares of you.

Class Info:

Once per fight, archers can shoot twice on one turn.

Name:

____

Race: Human

Class: Archer

Armor: 18

Health: 22

<u>Attack</u>

1d20+9 —> 1d10

Stuff:

Leather Armor, Bow

HUMAN ARCHER

Race Info:

Once per day you can make a **healing potion**, if you find medicinal herbs.

OR

Once per day you can use magic to **stun everyone** within two squares of you.

Class Info:

Once per fight, archers can shoot twice on one turn.

Name:

____

Race: Human

Class: Archer

Armor: 18

Health: 22

Attack

1d20+9 —> 1d10

Stuff:

Leather Armor, Bow

HUMAN BARBARIAN

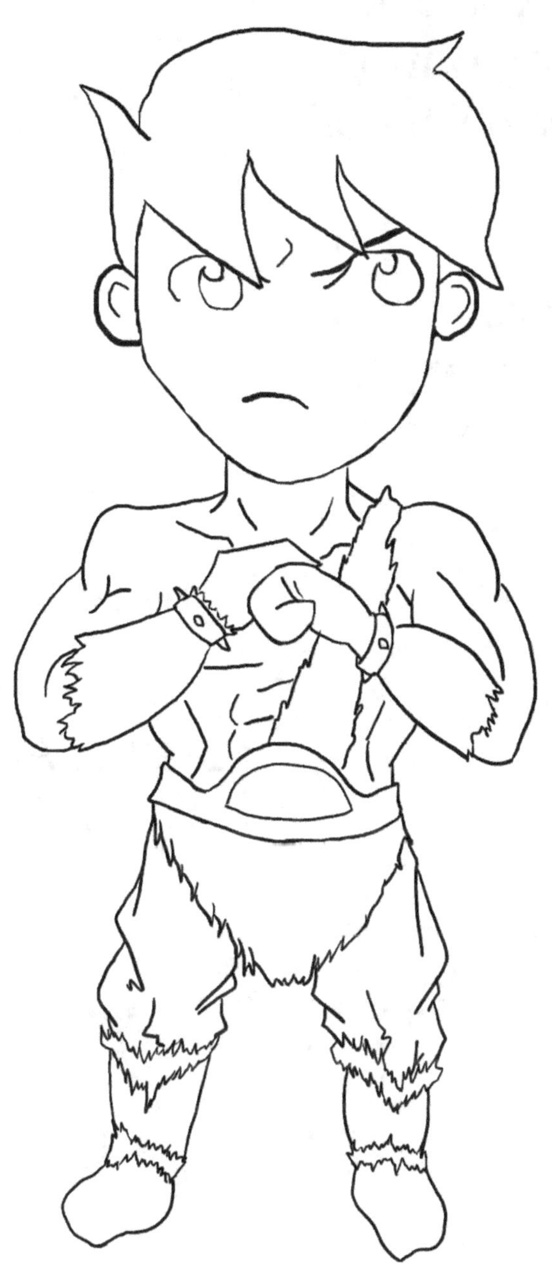

Race Info:

Once per day you can make a **healing potion**, if you find medicinal herbs.

OR

Once per day you can use magic to **stun everyone** within two squares of you.

Class Info:

-

Name:

____

Race: Human
Class: Barbarian
Armor: 17
Health: 31

Attack

1d20+8 —> 1d10+8

Stuff:

Leather Armor

HUMAN BARBARIAN

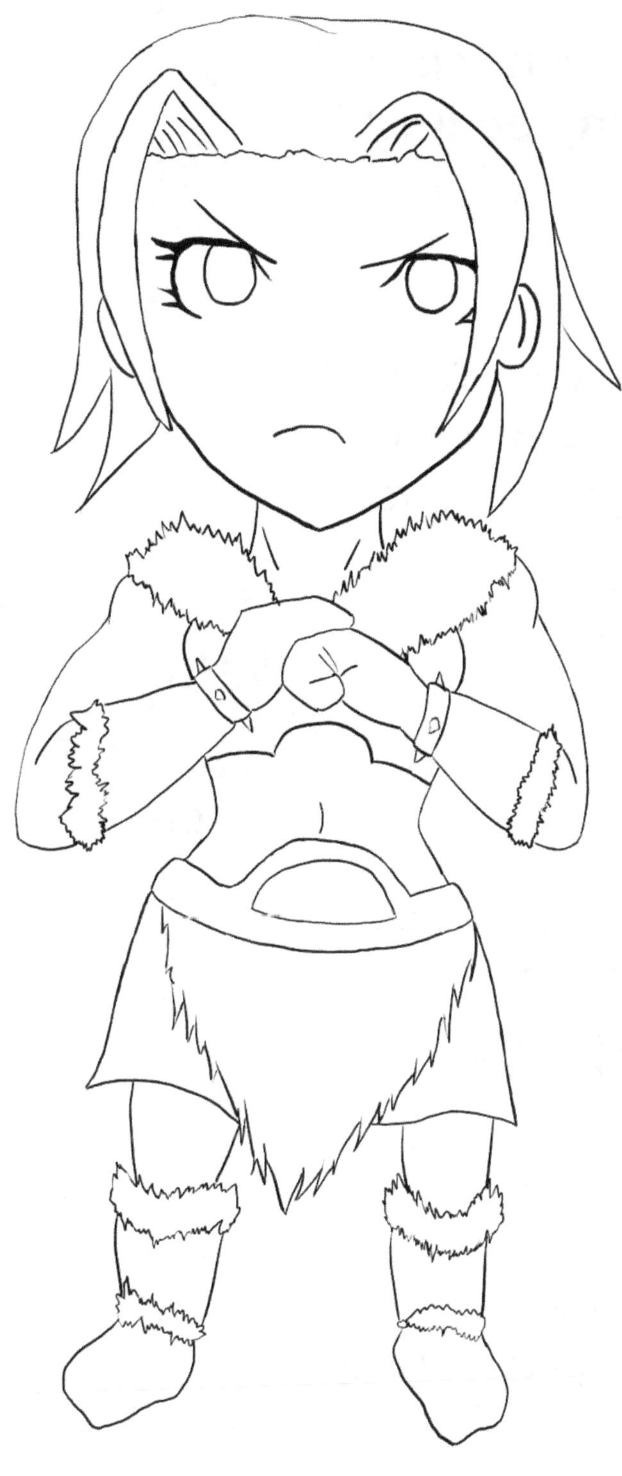

Race Info:

Once per day you can make a **healing potion**, if you find medicinal herbs.

OR

Once per day you can use magic to **stun everyone** within two squares of you.

Class Info:

_

Name:

Stuff:

Leather Armor

____

Race: Human
Class: Barbarian
Armor: 17
Health: 31
Attack
1d20+8 —> 1d10+8

HUMAN HEALER

____

Race Info:

Once per day you can make a **healing potion**, if you find medicinal herbs.

OR

Once per day you can use magic to **stun everyone** within two squares of you.

Class Info:

Instead of attacking, healers can **heal** a friend within 5 squares by **10 health.** You can do this **3 times per day.**

Name:

____

Race: Human

Class: Healer

Armor: 16

Health: 22

Attack

1d20+5 —> 1d8+3

Stuff:

Magic Jewel

HUMAN HEALER

____

Race Info:

Once per day you can make a **healing potion**, if you find medicinal herbs.

OR

Once per day you can use magic to **stun everyone** within two squares of you.

Class Info:

Instead of attacking, healers can **heal** a friend within 5 squares by **10 health.** You can do this **3 times per day.**

Name:

____

Race: Human
Class: Healer
Armor: 16
Health: 22

Stuff:

Magic Jewel

Attack

1d20+5 —> 1d8+3

HUMAN PALADIN

Race Info:

Once per day you can make a **healing potion**, if you find medicinal herbs.

OR

Once per day you can use magic to **stun everyone** within two squares of you.

Class Info:

Instead of attacking, paladins can **challenge** a bad guy next to them. That bad guy may only attack you and has to leave your friends alone. It lasts until you challenge someone else, or the fight ends.

Name:

____

Race: Human

Class: Paladin

Armor: 20

Health: 35

Attack

1d20+7 —> 1d8+3

Stuff:

Metal Armor, Sword

HUMAN THIEF

Race Info:

Once per day you can make a **healing potion**, if you find medicinal herbs.

OR

Once per day you can use magic to **stun everyone** within two squares of you.

Class Info:

If the bad guy you hit has one of your friends on the other side of it you get **backstab bonus, +2d6** extra damage.

Thieves are the only class that can **pick locks.**

Name:

____

Race: Human
Class: Thief
Armor: 16
Health: 23

Attack

1d20+8 —> 1d6+5

Stuff:

Leather Armor, Dagger, Lockpicks

HUMAN THIEF

Race Info:

Once per day you can make a **healing potion**, if you find medicinal herbs.

OR

Once per day you can use magic to **stun everyone** within two squares of you.

Class Info:

If the bad guy you hit has one of your friends on the other side of it you get **backstab bonus, +2d6** extra damage.

Thieves are the only class that can **pick locks.**

Name:

____

Race: Human
Class: Thief
Armor: 16
Health: 23

Attack

1d20+8 —> 1d6+5

Stuff:

Leather Armor, Dagger, Lockpicks

HUMAN WIZARD

Race Info:

Once per day you can make a **healing potion**, if you find medicinal herbs.

OR

Once per day you can use magic to **stun everyone** within two squares of you.

Class Info:

Instead of attacking, wizards can **curse** a bad guy up to 10 squares away. Cursed bad guys have

-2 armor and -2 damage for the rest of the fight.

Name:

____

Race: Human

Class: Wizard

Armor: 11

Health: 18

Attack

1d20+7 —> 1d6+5

+5 Splash Damage!

Stuff:

Robe, Staff, Big Feathered Hat

HUMAN WIZARD

Race Info:

Once per day you can make a **healing potion**, if you find medicinal herbs.

OR

Once per day you can use magic to **stun everyone** within two squares of you.

Class Info:

Instead of attacking, wizards can **curse** a bad guy up to 10 squares away. Cursed bad guys have **-2 armor and -2 damage** for the rest of the fight.

Name:

____

Race: Human

Class: Wizard

Armor: 11

Health: 18

Attack

1d20+7 —> 1d6+5

+5 Splash Damage!

Stuff:

Robe, Staff, Big Feathered Hat

Dwarf Archer

Race Info:	Class Info:
Dwarves get 7 extra Health. (Already added for you)	Once per fight, archers can shoot twice on one turn.

Name:	Stuff:
	Leather Armor, Bow

____

Race: Dwarf
Class: Archer
Armor: 18
Health: 29

Attack
1d20+9 —> 1d10

Dwarf Archer

Race Info:

Dwarves get 7 extra Health.
(Already added for you)

Class Info:

Once per fight, archers can shoot twice on one turn.

Name:

Stuff:

Leather Armor, Bow

____

Race: Dwarf
Class: Archer
Armor: 18
Health: 29
Attack
1d20+9 —> 1d10

Dwarf Barbarian

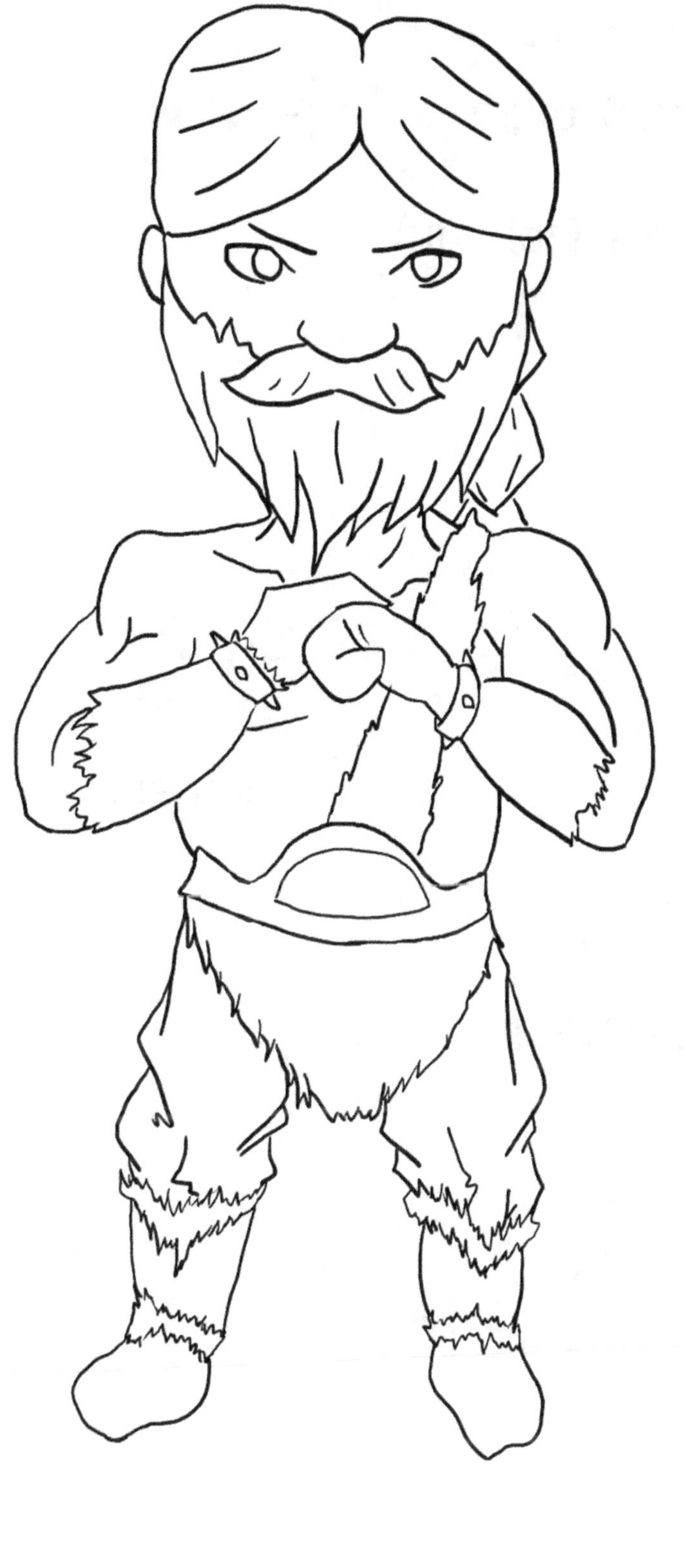

____

Race Info:	Class Info:
Dwarves get 7 extra Health. (Already added for you)	-

Name:	Stuff:
___________	Leather Armor

Race: Dwarf

Class: Barbarian

Armor: 17

Health: 38

<u>Attack</u>

1d20+8 —> 1d10+8

Dwarf Barbarian

Race Info:	Class Info:

Dwarves get 7 extra
Health.
(Already added for you)

-

Name:

Stuff:

Leather Armor

____

Race: Dwarf
Class: Barbarian
Armor: 17
Health: 38

<u>Attack</u>

1d20+8 —> 1d10+8

Dwarf Healer

Race Info:

Dwarves get 7 extra
Health.
(Already added for you)

Class Info:

Instead of attacking,
healers can **heal** a friend
within 5 squares by
10 health. You can do this
3 times per day.

Name:

Stuff:

Magic Jewel

____

Race: Dwarf
Class: Healer
Armor: 16
Health: 29
Attack
1d20+5 —> 1d8+3

Dwarf Healer

Race Info:

Dwarves get 7 extra Health.
(Already added for you)

Class Info:

Instead of attacking, healers can **heal** a friend within 5 squares by **10 health.** You can do this **3 times per day.**

Name:

Stuff:

Magic Jewel

____

Race: Dwarf
Class: Healer
Armor: 16
Health: 29
Attack
1d20+5 —> 1d8+3

Dwarf Paladin

Race Info:

Dwarves get 7 extra
Health.
(Already added for you)

Class Info:

Instead of attacking,
paladins can **challenge** a
bad guy next to them.
That bad guy may only
attack you and has to
leave your friends alone. It
lasts until you challenge
someone else, or the fight
ends.

Name:

____

Race: Dwarf
Class: Paladin
Armor: 20
Health: 42

Attack

1d20+7 —> 1d8+3

Stuff:

Metal Armor, Sword

Dwarf Paladin

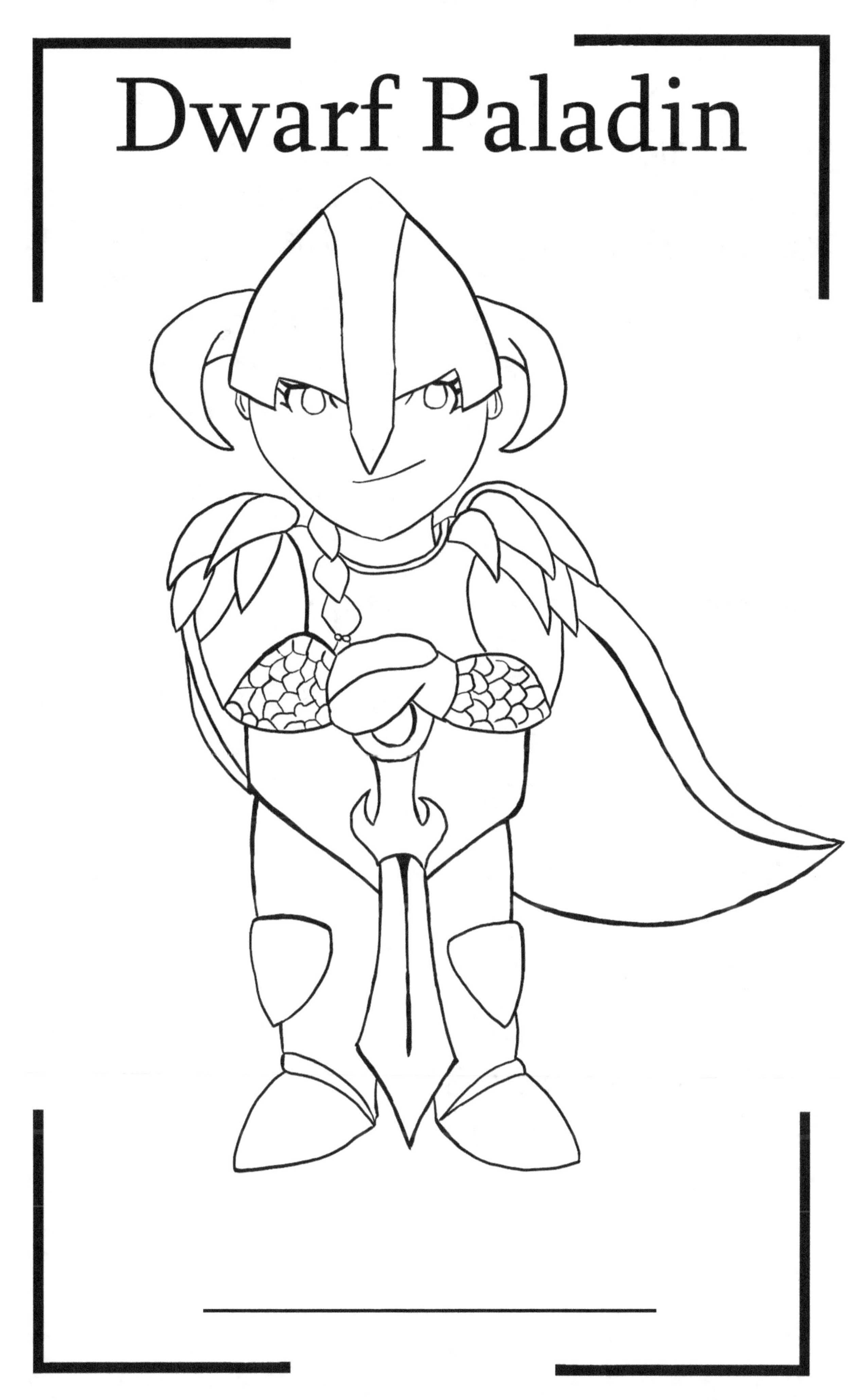

Race Info:

Dwarves get 7 extra Health.
(Already added for you)

Class Info:

Instead of attacking, paladins can **challenge** a bad guy next to them. That bad guy may only attack you and has to leave your friends alone. It lasts until you challenge someone else, or the fight ends.

Name:

Stuff:

Metal Armor, Sword

____

Race: Dwarf

Class: Paladin

Armor: 20

Health: 42

Attack

1d20+7 —> 1d8+3

Dwarf Thief

Race Info:

Dwarves get 7 extra
Health.
(Already added for you)

Class Info:

If the bad guy you hit has
one of your friends on the
other side of it you get
backstab bonus, +2d6
extra damage.

Thieves are the only class
that can **pick locks.**

Name:

Stuff:

Leather Armor, Dagger,
Lockpicks

____

Race: Dwarf
Class: Thief
Armor: 16
Health: 30
Attack
1d20+8 —> 1d6+5

Dwarf Thief

Race Info:

Dwarves get 7 extra Health.
(Already added for you)

Class Info:

If the bad guy you hit has one of your friends on the other side of it you get **backstab bonus, +2d6** extra damage.

Thieves are the only class that can **pick locks.**

Name:

____

Race: Dwarf

Class: Thief

Armor: 16

Health: 30

Attack

1d20+8 —> 1d6+5

Stuff:

Leather Armor, Dagger, Lockpicks

Dwarf Wizard

Race Info:

Dwarves get 7 extra
Health.
(Already added for you)

Class Info:

Instead of attacking,
wizards can **curse** a bad
guy up to 10 squares
away. Cursed bad guys
have
-2 armor and -2 damage
for the rest of the fight.

Name:

____

Race: Dwarf
Class: Wizard
Armor: 11
Health: 25

Attack

1d20+7 —> 1d6+5

Stuff:

Robe, Staff,
Big Feathered Hat

Dwarf Wizard

Race Info:

Dwarves get 7 extra
Health.
(Already added for you)

Class Info:

Instead of attacking,
wizards can **curse** a bad
guy up to 10 squares
away. Cursed bad guys
have
-2 armor and -2 damage
for the rest of the fight.

Name:

____

Race: Dwarf
Class: Wizard
Armor: 11
Health: 25

<u>Attack</u>
1d20+7 —> 1d6+5

Stuff:

Robe, Staff,
Big Feathered Hat

Halfling Archer

Race Info:

Once per fight, Halflings can make any bad guy that hit them re-roll that attack.

Class Info:

Once per fight, archers can shoot twice on one turn.

Name:

____

Race: Halfling
Class: Archer
Armor: 18
Health: 22

Attack
1d20+9 —> 1d10

Stuff:

Leather Armor, Bow

Halfling Archer

Race Info:

Once per fight, Halflings can make any bad guy that hit them re-roll that attack.

Class Info:

Once per fight, archers can shoot twice on one turn.

Name:

Stuff:

Leather Armor, Bow

____

Race: Halfling
Class: Archer
Armor: 18
Health: 22

Attack
1d20+9 —> 1d10

Halfling Barbarian

Race Info:

Once per fight, Halflings can make any bad guy that hit them re-roll that attack.

Class Info:

-

Name:

____

Race: Halfling
Class: Barbarian
Armor: 17
Health: 31
<u>Attack</u>
1d20+8 —> 1d10+8

Stuff:

Leather Armor

Halfling Barbarian

____

Race Info:

Once per fight, Halflings can make any bad guy that hit them re-roll that attack.

Class Info:

-

Name:

____

Race: Halfling
Class: Barbarian
Armor: 17
Health: 31
Attack
1d20+8 —> 1d10+8

Stuff:

Leather Armor

Halfling Healer

Race Info:

Once per fight, Halflings can make any bad guy that hit them re-roll that attack.

Class Info:

Instead of attacking, healers can **heal** a friend within 5 squares by **10 health.** You can do this **3 times per day.**

Name:

____

Race: Halfling
Class: Healer
Armor: 16
Health: 22

<u>Attack</u>
1d20+5 —> 1d8+3

Stuff:

Magic Jewel

Halfling Healer

Race Info:

Once per fight, Halflings can make any bad guy that hit them re-roll that attack.

Class Info:

Instead of attacking, healers can **heal** a friend within 5 squares by **10 health.** You can do this **3 times per day.**

Name:

____

Race: Halfling
Class: Healer
Armor: 16
Health: 22

Attack
1d20+5 —> 1d8+3

Stuff:

Magic Jewel

Halfling Paladin

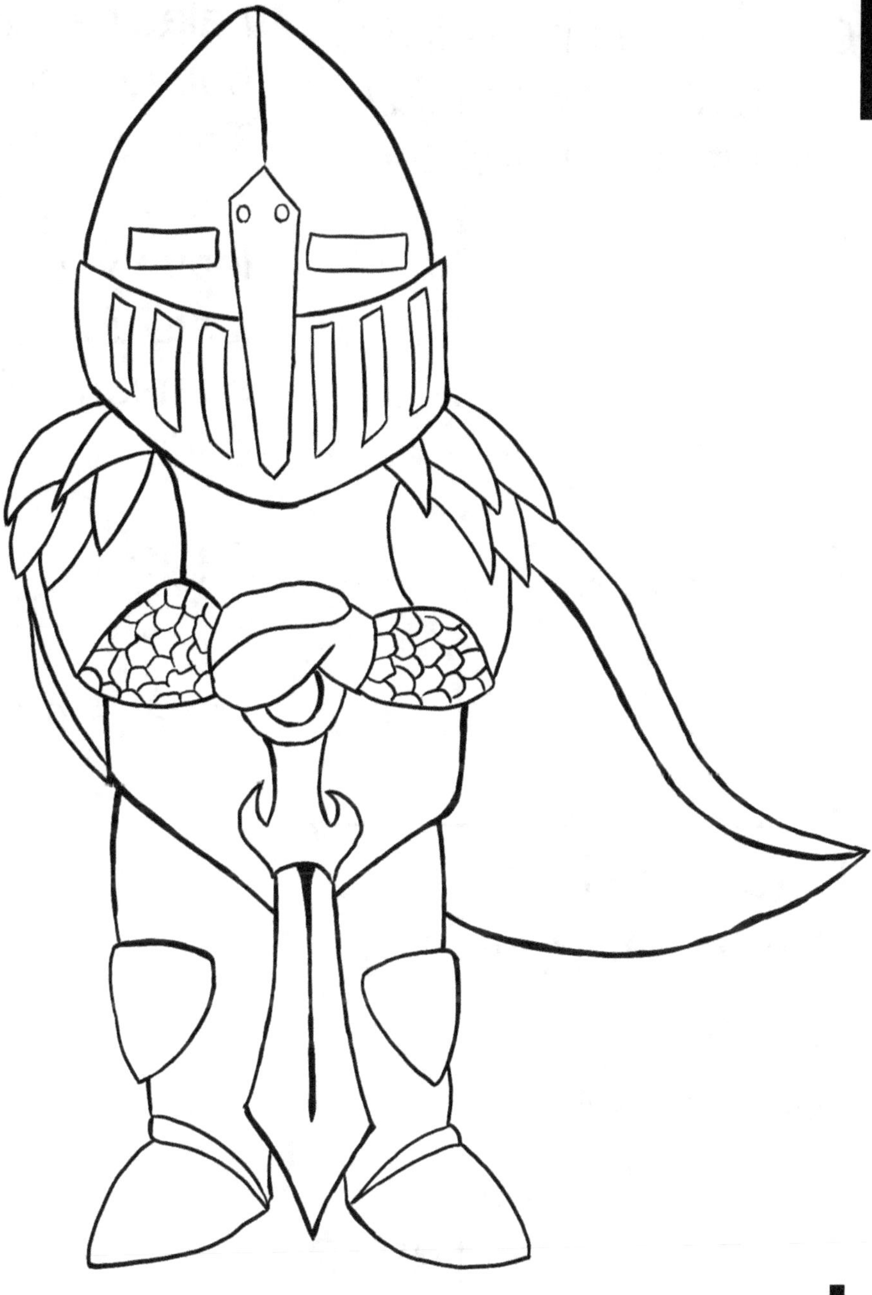

Race Info:

Once per fight, Halflings can make any bad guy that hit them re-roll that attack.

Class Info:

Instead of attacking, paladins can **challenge** a bad guy next to them. That bad guy may only attack you and has to leave your friends alone. It lasts until you challenge someone else, or the fight ends.

Name:

Stuff:

Metal Armor, Sword

____

Race: Halfling
Class: Paladin
Armor: 20
Health: 35

<u>Attack</u>
1d20+7 —> 1d8+3

Halfling Thief

Race Info:

Once per fight, Halflings can make any bad guy that hit them re-roll that attack.

Class Info:

If the bad guy you hit has one of your friends on the other side of it you get **backstab bonus, +2d6** extra damage.

Thieves are the only class that can **pick locks.**

Name:

____

Race: Halfling

Class: Thief

Armor: 16

Health: 23

<u>Attack</u>

1d20+8 —> 1d6+5

Stuff:

Leather Armor, Dagger, Lockpicks

Halfling Thief

Race Info:

Once per fight, Halflings can make any bad guy that hit them re-roll that attack.

Class Info:

If the bad guy you hit has one of your friends on the other side of it you get **backstab bonus, +2d6** extra damage.

Thieves are the only class that can **pick locks.**

Name:

____

Race: Halfling

Class: Thief

Armor: 16

Health: 23

Attack

1d20+8 —> 1d6+5

Stuff:

Leather Armor, Dagger, Lockpicks

Halfling Wizard

Race Info:

Once per fight, Halflings can make any bad guy that hit them re-roll that attack.

Class Info:

Instead of attacking, wizards can **curse** a bad guy up to 10 squares away. Cursed bad guys have

-2 armor and -2 damage for the rest of the fight.

Name:

____

Race: Halfling

Class: Wizard

Armor: 11

Health: 18

Attack

1d20+7 —> 1d6+5

+5 Splash Damage!

Stuff:

Robe, Staff,
Big Feathered Hat

Halfling Wizard

Race Info:

Once per fight, Halflings can make any bad guy that hit them re-roll that attack.

Class Info:

Instead of attacking, wizards can **curse** a bad guy up to 10 squares away. Cursed bad guys have
-2 armor and -2 damage for the rest of the fight.

Name:

____

Race: Halfling

Class: Wizard

Armor: 11

Health: 18

Attack

1d20+7 —> 1d6+5

+5 Splash Damage!

Stuff:

Robe, Staff,
Big Feathered Hat

ABOUT THE AUTHOR

NICK BAER is a hard-working, dedicated family man with a passion for gaming—both table top and video games. He has played games since a very young age, and now enjoys sharing his passion with his daughter, Clara and his fiance, Katie.

In 2012, he began his martial arts journey at Sun Yi's Academy of Tae Kwon Do in Arcata, CA where he met Travis Holter, and forged a friendship that evolved into a collaborative partnership to create table top modules.

Nick is now pursuing his childhood dream of becoming an artist, along with enjoying his new-found love for martial arts. His work can be found at lordnickage.deviantart.com, doomdojo.com and facebook.com/thelordbaeron.